Living with Agenda 21

Living with Agenda 21

Surrendering Our Freedoms

Dr. H. Lawrence Zillmer

To order additional copies of this book, contact:
Xlibris Corporation
1-888-795-4274
www.Xlibris.com
Orders@Xlibris.com
122063

TABLE OF CONTENTS

PROLOGUE

You will have a hard time believing what you are about to read! What is this Agenda 21? It is a United Nations "agenda!" Never heard of it! By design of those who would implement it! It can't happen in good old U.S.A.! It already has! Bill Clinton made it federal policy by Executive Order 12858 in 1993! How will this affect me? As Pelosi said about Obamacare, "Pass it and you'll find out!"

Is this all some alarmist "conspiracy" theory. All anyone needs to do is go to Wikipedia and type in Agenda 21 and read all about it. Throughout the work various other sources will be cited. Check them out.

The fact is that the Obama administration is working through the czars and his executive orders to hurry this process through before the American voters even know what happened. Part of it is Obamacare which affects one sixth of the American economy. We are discovering the truth about that program! Cap and Trade was defeated but it is being carried out by executive orders anyway. All this circumvents the American Congress, the Constitution and the Bill of rights—it is a U.N. program facilitated by NGOs (Non-Government Organizations) and MOAs, (Memorandums Of Agreement). They already exist in every state in our nation. Four cities in Texas, beginning with Houston, have Agenda 21 groups! Why? Money! Incredible money can be made by a one-world government, one currency, with all property owned by the government!

It is time we recognize U.N. Agenda 21, its motive, its goal and the final result, should we allow it to happen. They have already achieved part of their agenda. Check it out and allow your disgust and fury to stir you into action.

Agenda 21

When in the course of human affairs several streams of thought, like tributaries to a river, flow together, the result is either of great benefit for those using the resources of the resulting river, or a disastrous flood, destructive and destroying. We are witnessing the latter.

A United Nations conference in Rio de Janeiro in 1992, brought together concerns for our environment, Socialism, Secular Humanism, and the world banking cartels. The result was Agenda 21. This program was unanimously approved and implemented by the United Nations. President George H. W. Bush called Agenda 21 "sacred principles" and called on all Americans to pledge allegiance to those same principles. As stated earlier, it became policy through Executive Order 12858, issued in 1993 by President Bill Clinton.

Our current president is dedicated to implementing Agenda 21 through his executive orders directed by his 50 plus "Czars." The programs formulated by Agenda 21 are in place and is policy today. Current governmental policies are dedicated to carrying out Agenda 21.

At this moment the United States army is training U. N. troops, called the "Blue Helmets," at bases in our country. The Blue Helmets have already been used to quell a riot in Chicago in May, 2012. Abandoned army training bases, ostensibly reserved by FEMA for emergency housing for times of a national emergency, are reequipped for housing anyone convicted of a "hate crime," defined as speaking against governmental policies.

As of this writing, thousands of NGOs exist nationwide. Four Texas cities have specific organizations dedicated to carrying out the programs of Agenda 21. Tyler is one of them. The Tyler group is named Tyler 21.

PART ONE

What is Agenda 21?

The simple reality is that we have in operation in the United States a policy formed by the United Nations, a policy most people have never heard of, guided and being implemented by the executive branch of our Federal Government. It is time we awoke to what this means to each of us, learn what it is all about, and then deal with it according to the will of the people. We the people have a right to choose who and what shall govern us. Let us begin by examining what it is and how it arrived in our lives. As indicted, four channels of human thinking coalesced into Agenda 21: Environmentalism, Socialism, Secular Humanism and the banking cartels.

Environmentalism.

Following World War II we began to truly awaken to various environmental problems. Water pollution, air pollution, land wastage, denuded rainforests, vanishing species of plant and animal life and perceived overpopulation drew the attention and became grist for the press, especially the alarmist press. It sells news! "Going Green" became a byword for this new concern about our environment.

The human stewardship of our island planet is a given. No animal or plant would befoul or destroy its own nest! No thinking person could deny the environmental problems facing ourselves and our children.

Socialism.

Beginning in the 19th century, the ground swell of anger over the abuse of workers by industrial moguls surged into our newspapers and public media. Wealthy capitalists owned and controlled the means of living. In too many cases greed and power were exercised at the expense of the laborers who produced the products of wealth.

Men and women, such as Karl Marx, Friedrich Engels, Robert Owen and Mary Wollstonecraft wrote of the need to share more equally the wealth from production and commerce. Among the many "isms," Communism, Socialism and Fascism rose into prominence, each advocating a means of sharing the wealth. Communism would eliminate the owners and turn their capitalistic enterprises over to the government for management. Socialism has the same agenda but would achieve the control of the economy by a different means. Fabian socialism became the avenue for achieving total control of a society. The Fabians believed that by anonymity and subterfuge they could gradually replace the middle class owners through governmental manipulation, which would result in control and eventual ownership. Fascism is but another name for the same control of the means of production and control of a society. Hitler's Nazi party was officially named The Socialist Workers Party.

The goal of Socialism in any form is big government capable of controlling every aspect of human living. By this control they believe that they can achieve "Sustainable Development," the watchword of socialism. Ideologues, versed in Communism/ Socialism, would lead the people into this ideal planned society. Sustainable Development, as exercised by ideologues, would protect and ration the use of the environment in such a manner as to protect it, sustain it and share it equally. Since many of the representatives to the U. N. conference in Rio de Janeiro came from countries already under the direction of Fabian Socialism, the resulting Agenda 21 is a Socialist's program of how to ration the resources derived from the environment and thereby obtaining "sustainable development."

Anyone opposing this socialist view of the environment became an enemy of the people. They were not being willing to give to the common good and therefore committing a "hate crime." The ideologues promoted the logic tight argument that their program and none other was for the good of the people. The argument developed that to reject the Socialist view was to be an enemy of the people, a criminal, a destroyer of our planet. Since by that argument the capitalistic system promoted personal use of the environment, they were easily labeled enemies of the people, the definition of which depended upon the teachings and the power of the various ideologues. Environmental concerns welded neatly into the socialist goals—Agenda 21.

Secular Humanism

Beginning in the 16th century, mankind began to shake off the idea that a priesthood determined truth in all fields of inquiry. "Man is the measure of all things," including religion. This became modern philosophy. Man determined what was truth and what was not. The scientific movement morphed into this attitude. What need was there for a Deity to tell us what we needed to do or say? We can figure it out for ourselves! Whatever Deity exists, if any, is determined by who or what we believe the Deity to be!

The formula for truth in the church from its beginning was based upon the three revelations of the Deity: In the Natural Laws of this creation, in the life and teachings of Jesus and in the ministry of the Holy Spirit, which focused upon what was sin, what was God's standard of righteousness and what was the basis of God's judgment of human behavior. Therefore, because this revelation came from God, was based upon Natural Law, it is to be humbly listened to. It was truth by which to live—diametrically opposed to the Socialist view!

The Natural Law is summarized in the Ten Commandments: (1) There is only one system of laws in this Creation. (2) Do not make any human substitutes. (3) Do not count God's revelations as nothing. (4) Take time out for spiritual development. (5) Honor those who have gone before us, beginning with our parents. (6) You shall do no murder. (7) You shall guard and protect the family by not committing adultery, fornication, or homosexuality. (8) You shall not steal. (9) You shall not lie. (10) You shall not covet what is another's. Jesus added the necessary motivation for living in harmony with Natural Law through His commandment, "You shall love one another as I have loved you." (John 13:34, 15:12, 17)

This has been the standard of Judeo-Christianity down through the centuries. It is not to say that it was always followed but the standard was there when Christians were faithful to their roots. Anyone could commit to this way of life, not by vows of poverty, chastity and obedience, but by doing acts of love—caring, responding to real need, respecting and understanding the individual. By the beginning of the modern era the church had strayed far from its original mission, leaving Christianity wide open for criticism. Since it was believed that man is the measure of all things, new denominations proliferated, including atheism. Skepticism returned to the fore with its idea that since no one could agree as to what was truth, absolute truth did not exist! This assumed that man could determine what was absolute truth and what was not!

Men, such as Freud, taught that religion had served its purpose and was no longer needed. Carried further, Lenin said that religion was the opiate of the people. Reformed theologians disagreed among themselves as to truth, but were united in the belief that what they thought to be truth was actually truth, and they could go to the Christian Bible and find proof for their ascertains.

Different denominations increased in number year by year. The strife and even killings between religions only proved to many that religion was indeed something we could do without. In the heady notions that man is the measure of all things, solipsism, the idea that what we believe is truth is truth because we believe it, developed. Coupled with narcissism, solipsism became a mighty force in the world of theology.

For many the new religion was environmentalism. Saving the planet through socialist ideals was the highest good. The stage was set for the fourth of the "tributaries" of our current "river."

The Banking Cartel.

Money has been the medium of exchange since human beings traded worth for worth. With the discovery and rapid development of America, the need of money for development became acute. Banks developed which offered capital in exchange for interest payments for the use of the money. New lands, railroads, projects, highways, all demanded capital, which banks were willing to loan—for a fee! Where did they get the money to loan? Ultimately they simply printed it!

The history of banking in America is a history of highs and depressions, many banks going into default through bad lending practices. In 1913 a group of very wealthy financiers met in secret on the Jekyl Island retreat of the Morgan family to form some means of getting better control of money through a better banking system. The result of that meeting was the Federal Reserve System. The shareholders are a banking cartel using the name of "Federal" in order to sound important. They are not a branch of the Federal Government!

Over the years they acquired more and more money and therefore power. Wars are very profitable! So profitable that, following World War II, wider horizons beckoned for the world's financiers. The World Bank and the International Monetary Fund developed. The Bilderberg Group was formed. All dedicated to a one world government and a single currency—Agenda 21.

The stage was set for the unholy alliance of politicians needing more money than they had for various "entitlements," which the people wanted. By giving them the entitlements they wanted they were assured of getting the recipient's vote. Every dollar loaned to the government by the various banking cartels meant income from that loan in the form of interest payments for the shareholders! The more debt, the more interest, so the more income! It didn't matter if the loans were never paid off—that would cost the financiers income! It is important to remember that every dollar of increased debt, for whatever reason (and skillful politicians can find many reasons), is money in the pockets of the financiers!

Wars, even little ones, were falling into distaste but a new avenue for political profit opened up in the welfare state. Financing wars in Iraq and Afghanistan weren't providing enough income, but who could be against helping out the poor? Isn't that our Christian duty? Loans to support welfare programs ballooned. Each aid program meant increased indebtedness and therefore more money for the financiers. When people began to sour on the abuse of welfare by some, a new avenue must be found for the politicians and the financiers to exploit for profit. Enter environmentalism! Income from small wars, welfare programs and various environmental projects guarantee that debts will never be paid off, which means assured income for the shareholders of the banking cartels.

So began the unholy alliance of mostly well-meaning environmentalists, socialists, secular humanism and the banking cartels. The resulting program is Agenda 21. The result of implementing Agenda 21 is staggering debt, the interest of which must be paid to the financiers before there is any money left for the goods and services human societies need, increasing governmental control of every facet of life, governmental control of all property and businesses and a "dumbing down" of our educational system provides subservient workers for the system. The cynical use of small wars to protect the nation (Afghanistan), welfare and the environment, by the politicians and the bankers, guarantee a debt our grandchildren will never pay off! Furthermore every dollar spent in servicing the interest payments means that much less money is not available for current expenses. At this time more that half of the national income is spent servicing the financiers before any other need can be addressed. Let us now look at the details of this insidious program, what is being implemented in our societies, although most people have never heard of Agenda 21, even as it slowly but surely strangles our resources and our freedoms.

PART TWO

The Goals of Agenda 21.

It is critical to remember that Agenda 21 is a <u>United Nations</u> program. It did not originate through the legislative channels of the United States. It is therefore not part of our judicial system, except when various local, state or federal laws are passed regarding it. Therefore anyone attempting to use our court system for redress or complaint, as a result of Agenda 21 practices, will discover that the case has "no standing." Since Agenda 21 is not part of the system, no redress can be adjudicated by our judicial system!

The original Agenda 21 was passed by the United Nations. The American delegation voted for it. Several conferences have been held subsequently to fine tune the system. There is one going on right now (Rio + 20 Earth Summit) celebrating twenty years of "progress" in implementing the program. As indicated earlier, Agenda 21 passed into usage into our governmental system via executive order. It has never passed through our legislative or judicial system. It remains a protocol agreed to by our delegates and supported by our membership in the United Nations. It operates entirely apart from our representative governmental system.

The forces behind Agenda 21 are as old as humanity, indeed as old as the first human being. Following the pattern of Natural Law, offspring are nurtured until they are old enough to fend for themselves. The offspring either uses what they have learned and survives, or, if they aren't able to adjust to the world outside of their mother, they die.

So it is with humans. After a lengthy childhood ranging into their teens, children are expected to lead their own lives, make their own decisions and be responsible for their decisions, erroneous or wise.

But what if a child does not want to assume personal responsibility? What if they want to continue as a dependent, with others making decisions for them? Whole societies have this problem. It is described in the Bible.

A time came when the Israelites were tired of making their own decisions based upon the Ten Commandments. They wanted a king to make the tough decisions for them. Samuel described what would happen to them if they had a king. (I Samuel 8:1-22) The king would tax them, take their young men into his army, select the most beautiful girls for himself and his aides and both he, his queen and his favorites would spend money lavishly. They insisted on having a king, and their kings, being humans with power, did exactly what Samuel had told them would happen.

Over two hundred years ago our forefathers got rid of a king. They believed they could rule themselves in harmony with Natural Law and its Creator. It worked. It turned loose the creative energy of a people willing to work.

We don't have many kings anymore, but the drive to allow others to have autocratic control is still very much with us. Replace "kings" with "ideologues" and you have our situation today.

We have a representative form of government.

We elect men and women who will manage our affairs but whom we can turn out when they don't. The system has worked very well. We must remember, we have a "representative" system of government based upon our Federal Constitution. This system works when its citizens are willing to understand choices, study the men and women who would represent them, and express their wishes through responsible ballots.

In our times a new aristocracy has arisen—ideologues, men and women who believe they know how to run societies and make everyone bow to their wills, which they believe is an expression of the "common good." Why? They say it's for the good of this planet but is it really? Enormous sums of money are available for the taking by those who can somehow get themselves promoted into leadership!

Chiefs, kings, emperors and queens and ideologues can live very well, better than the average person. Furthermore they don't have to labor—work; they can have others do it for them. So we have seen ideologues rising into power who have never really worked physically, nor could they ever make their way in the world of commerce. As far as society is concerned they are of little benefit for they produce nothing. But if by one means or another they can rise to power, they can live like kings and queens off the labor of others. They are the new achievers, people who could not, in many cases, earn a working person's wages, but now are dispensing their ideas by force, being eulogized as saviors and therefore living well.

Take for instance Obamacare. It is managed by people who could not make a living in the medical field. Yet their decisions are absolute. One is fined if they do not jump through hoops created by ignorant bureaucrats. This pattern is repeated in every area of economic endeavor under Socialism.

The entire implementation of Agenda 21 in the United States is carried out by non-elected bureaucrats, such as the "czars" of the current administration, and by executive order. It completely ignores the legislative and legal processes. President Obama has issued over nine hundred executive orders, most in some way impacting the implementation of Agenda 21. I shall deal with specific details of these orders in Part Three.

Agenda 21 operates behind a green mask

It is an environmental cover-up for socialist programs. Many people are caught up in the Going Green idea. Under the environmental cover the socialist programs can be fine tuned. When questioned, who can argue against saving our planet!

Well heeled proponents of the socialist program, who will become very wealthy and influential through administering Agenda 21, provide a hard core of advocates for the program. Men like Saul Alinsky, advocate radical action, as in his book, "Rules for Radicals," the first edition of which he dedicated to Lucifer, who "through rebellion gained a kingdom." Men, such as George Soros, spend millions supporting various cell organizations throughout the United

States and grow wealthy through it! None of this is done publically. It is all in accord with the processes of Fabian Socialism.

Implementation of Agenda 21 depends upon MOAs (Memorandums of Agreement) and NGOs (Non-governmental Organizations). Non-elected and unaccountable nongovernmental regional planning bodies, in collaboration with appointed Federal officials from various bureaus also not elected and therefore not accountable, meet to develop the program of Agenda 21. They agree to a program, but put little down on paper. It is a primarily a verbal contract, an MOA.

As soon as an elected body of government agrees to whatever program is suggested by some NGO, and they all sound perfectly innocent, the power of implementing the program passes out of the elected official's hands. An NGO is running the show through a MOA which, if a paper trail existed, could be traced all the way back to the United Nations. Much of our foreign aid is, at this moment, handled through this system. Committees by the hundreds are formed to implement various programs, suggested by Fabian Socialists, but when approved are handled by Agenda 21 personnel. Someone from the committees represents the Agenda cell and becomes the funnel through which money and power passes. Once the initial program is executed, grants are applied for and issued to the NGO. Now they have more real money in which to operate. None of it is on official record. All is behind the Green Mask; and it is extremely lucrative!

An example is the East Texas Council of Government. As the Federal Reserve Banking cartel has no official ties to the Federal government, so this "East Texas Council of Government" has no official ties to an elected government. A County Commissioner explained how it works.

Through an MOA, the money sent from the Texas treasury for use by the counties, in this case Smith County, is no longer dispersed by the County Commissioners. That "work" is handed over to the East Texas Council of Government. They disperse the money to those they deem "worthy." It is estimated that 40% of the money goes for "salaries and expenses" of the ETCG. So nearly half of what is collected by taxes and dispersed by the state government, goes into the pockets of this NGO. Since they are not elected, taxpayers have no control over how they disperse what is left of the state grant.

If someone has the money and the power they can buy into the Agenda 21 system and are allowed to organize a cell. They will then find supporters who will engage in the "Green Mask" patterns of promoting various environmental projects as a screen.

When they feel they can swing it, they will use elected sheriffs, etc, to push projects such as getting rid of religious artifacts, such as plaques of the Ten Commandments, or Creche scenes at Christmas. They will use whatever communication avenues are usable to promote the protection of endangered species, often to the slowing down or eliminating critical oil or mining practices. Appropriate groups can then do the actual prosecution of broken laws. They will act as a local vigilante group recording and reporting anything that they perceive is contrary to the implementation of Agenda 21 in their community.

Private / Public Partnerships

All this is obnoxious enough but one of their main objects in gaining power is so they can form Public/Private Partnerships (PPP) with various contractors and other business "friends." Crony capitalism! Through connections, various building and renovation projects are done without their having to go through the bidding process. The ability to swing contracts gives these NGOs groups tremendous economic leverage. NGOs like the East Texas Council of Government have a great deal of money to disperse. They become a PPP with whomever will work with them. Implementing Agenda 21 policies is very profitable to the members of the NGOs!

That is how a foreign agenda, formulated by the United Nations, is interjected into American society. To tell people what is in Agenda 21 is to be politically incorrect, a hate crime! People are simply not aware of the slow implementation of the agenda which benefits the implementers so lavishly while they actually produce nothing!

Silently but with absolute control and direction, our children are taught the Socialist agenda. As of this moment the children in public schools in Superior, Wisconsin, pledge their allegiance to the world, not to the United States.

Most of the Stimulus Money was spent on enlarging the executive branch of the government. Big government, government that will ultimately control every facet of our lives, is the pronounced goal. When President Obama spoke of entrepreneurs not creating jobs but that government was responsible for those jobs, he spoke the heart of socialist doctrine.

The goal of Communism was achieved in Russia, China, Cambodia and Cuba, through killing or imprisoning those who owned the factories and means of production. That is but one way of achieving the Socialist goals. Fabian Socialism intends to achieve those same goals without murdering the owners of farms and businesses. Through governmental regulations and taxes they expect to strangle American industrial might, which is then turned over to governmental bureaucrats to run, as in General Motors. It is all so very profitable!

It is like the proverbial frog in water on a stove. Turn up the heat a little at a time and eventually there will be boiled frog without the frog knowing it is being cooked! The reality is that Agenda 21, a program of the United Nations, is in place, it is governmental policy and we are on the receiving end of those practices. THIS IS NOT CONJECTURE, THIS IS ALREADY PART OF OUR LIVES!

Agenda 21 works for so many people in that it keeps them in a safe, controlled and seemingly secure box. They are allowed to develop their potential only if they act in accord with the "plan!" The key word is "communityism." Citizens surrender their individuality to a controlled and controlling community monitored by bureaucrats under the leadership of ideologues backed by the police, the Blue Helmets of the United Nations.

Like the ancient Israelites, too many people want someone to make the tough decisions for them. Kings are out of fashion but smart, intelligent and glib-tongued ideologues are not. People are willing to trade their individualism for security even if it is constrictive at times.

Whole religions, such as Buddhism, as well as all socialists regard individualism as "maya," evil. Yet we know that every human is different from every other human. Society will either support the development of that uniqueness as part of a larger whole, with society benefiting by the unity of diversity, or attempt to squelch it, also in the name of the common good—as in the socialist program behind the Green Mask.

Beyond all the philosophizing the simple fact is that controlling ideologues, by whatever name, get very wealthy. When wealth is centered in a few it means that the many have less. Through whatever justification, whatever social theories, whatever jingoes, propaganda, the ideologues get very rich; they exercise tremendous power and they love it! Most ideologues could not get rich through the normal channels of hard work and self discipline. But by being the idea people, by believing themselves to be smarter than the run of humanity, they believe they have the right to wealthy living.

In order to accomplish the goals of Agenda 21, a huge federal bureaucracy is necessary. The larger the country the more bureaucrats are needed. It is important to remember that government produces nothing except regulations and punishments for those not obeying the regulations. Therefore every dollar given to government is a dollar subtracted from what could be used to produce goods and services.

The only real beneficiary in all this are the banking cartels, the politicians, the ideologues and their bureaucrats who work to implement the policies. Regardless of what is regulated or stimulated or supported it all costs money.

The Law of the Spent Dollar.

It is an economic law that every dollar spent by the governmental bureaucrats is money not usable by individuals for economic growth. Money cannot be spent twice! Every dollar borrowed by the politicians for entitlements and various "pork barrel projects," means profits for the politician and the banking cartels. Every dollar borrowed must be subtracted from later income when the principal plus interest must be paid. This produces a need for further borrowing. It is money subtracted from what could be used to benefit the men and women of our economy. *It is stealing from our children and grandchildren to meet perceived present wants and needs.*

Socialism seeks governmental control of all means of production, transportation, communication, medicine, education, energy, housing, the environment and population. Agenda 21 ideologues must set aside our Constitution, with its Bill of Rights, with its focus on individualism and representative government. They will say it is outmoded, no longer needed in a progressive society. Communityism must replace individualism!

The point of all this struggle is humanity: Are we individuals who live our lives guided by a moral code, or are we but a cipher in some bureaucrat's computer to be manipulated for the good of the community according to the dictates of wealthy ideologues? Let us now look at specific programs and issues of Agenda 21.

PART THREE

Specific programs and issues

Let us examine the programs of Agenda 21 under those nine headings mentioned above: industrial and agricultural production, medicine, energy, education, housing, transportation, communication, the environment and population control. The stated goal of Agenda 21 is "sustainable production," that is, the Socialist idea of what we must do to continue to live well on our planet. I shall begin with the key Socialist issue, the means of livelihood—industry, business and agriculture.

1. <u>The control of production.</u>

We need to remember that the point and goal of the socialist policies under Agenda 21 is to get rid of the middle class, those who own the factories, businesses and farm lands. Under communism they are simply killed or jailed. Fabian Socialism has the same goals, but uses different means to achieve it. The end is the same, governmental control and regulation of every means of earning a living.

Why use firing squads when taxes and regulations produce income for more governmental projects, as well as pay the administrators of those projects. Tax the income of the capitalist and spread the "take" around to the oppressed workers! Under the new system, workers do the work and the new aristocracy of ideologues get the benefit—all for the common good!

Of course to do this tax collectors, tax laws and ever increasing number of bureaucrats are required. More and more regulations are needed. Businesses are spending incredible amounts of time filling out governmental forms which require ever increasing bureaucratic levels of administration. Taxes must increase to pay for it all! The end is to strangle private enterprise so it reverts to the government.

Government bailouts mean greater controls over those being bailed out. The auto industry, big banks and Fannie and Freddie Mack, are "too big to fail," but who wants them to fail when they can be controlled for profit for the bureaucrats? Private businesses are tolerated as long as they fill out the forms and pay their taxes! Absolute control has not yet been achieved but the Fabian processes are in full swing and working very well toward the Socialist goals. Ask any business man!

How about agriculture, the means of feeding the population? Here Socialism has had a sorry record. The collective farms of the Ukraine under communism, drained the agricultural production of one of the richest farmlands on earth. The Ukraine had little food for export until they allowed farmers to have a small plot of land to raise food for themselves. Why are collective farms such a failure?

Again, non-farmers were trying to tell farmers how to farm! Inexperienced farm laborers were to work together for a common goal! Between mismanagement and the unskilled workers who resented the work, little happened! In order to farm one must love the land and work very hard in sync with nature to raise a crop! A farmer must be motivated and free to use his or her skills in harmony with nature. Since, under Socialism, all land is owned by the government and all decisions are made by the government, where is the motive for the necessary hard labor of farming? As indicated, the track record of Socialism in feeding the populace is sorry indeed.

Add to this the concept of "biodiversity." According to this key idea of Agenda 21, all land is to be returned to its pristine original. According to their Biodiversity Assessment Document the following is to be reduced or eliminated: Ski runs (p. 337), grazing of livestock (p. 350), disturbing the soil surface by plowing (p. 351), using fossil fuels (p. 728), "human-made caves of brick and mortar" (homes) (p. 730), paved and tarred roads (p. 730), logging activities (748), dams and reservoirs (p. 755), power line construction (p. 757), and any and all economic systems that fail to meet governmental standards (p. 763).

Isn't it amazing what ideologues can dream up when they avoid reality? Again, all land is owned by the government and controlled by governmental bureaucrats who drain from the economy that which could be used to build the economy. Furthermore, the price of food skyrockets, except for the ideologues! Socialism has never worked because ideologues do not know and have no personal motivation other than control the livelihood of the people for their own benefit.

2. Medicine.

The struggle of the Obama administration to gain control of the medical field, one-sixth of the economy, is well documented. "Pass the legislation and you'll find out what's in it," said Speaker of the House Nancy Pelosi. And supposedly responsible legislators passed this several thousand page document mostly unread! Now we are finding out what it is they passed!

Judge Kithil of Marble Falls, Texas, has examined the voluminous Obama Health Care bill and here are some of the results:

Page 50, Section 152: The bill provides insurance to all non-U.S. citizens, even if they are here illegally.

Pages 58, 59: The government has real-time access to an individual's bank account and has authority to make electronic fund transfers from those accounts.

Page 65, Section 164: The plan subsidizes all union members, union retirees, and community organizations (such as ACORN).

Page 203, lines 14 and 15: The tax imposed under this bill will not be regarded as a tax!

Pages 241 and 253: Doctors will all be paid the same regardless of specialty, and the government will set all doctor's fees.

Page 272, section 1145: Cancer hospitals will ration care according to the patient's age.

Page 425, lines 4-12: The government mandates advance-care planning consultations. Those on Social Security will be required to attend an "end-of-life planning seminar" every five years.

Page 429, lines 13-25: The government will specify which doctors can write an end-of-life order.

This universal health care coverage will cost additional billions every year. How is this money to be acquired? It will be obtained by requiring young people, who don't usually need health care, to pay or be fined, and by eliminating most of the elderly who need it through euthanasia. In addition there will be increased taxes, which will hit the middle class hardest. The boundary seems to be 75 years of age. At this moment some dialysis patients have already been refused treatment because they are over 75. Euthanasia is now part of governmental population control program, as practiced in China. Population control, one of the nine goals of Socialism, will be discussed below.

Babies are to be micro-chipped so they can be traced throughout their lives. From the cradle to the grave the governmental bureaucrats now control all health care, all doctors, all hospitals, the dispensing of all medicines and all insurance plans. Where is the individual in all this? They no longer exist! They are only a cipher in the socialist state.

3. Energy.

One wonders why a president discourages drilling for needed oil and vetoes a Keystone Pipeline which will provide needed oil energy and jobs. Why all the emphasis on renewable energy sources which can never meet but a fraction of our energy needs? Each wind turbine will produce enough electricity in its life time to pay for its construction! It makes no sense unless one looks at the energy portion of Agenda 21.

Under the guise of "Sustainable Development," the reality that current resources of petroleum will eventually run out are manipulated to implement Agenda 21. People, whom Lenin called the "useful tools" of the revolution, have staged so many marches and made so many environmental law suits that atomic energy production has not further developed. So what other answer is there? Ration energy by governmental control. How? By emphasizing our "carbon footprint" and the means to reduce it through Cap and Trade legislation.

This impacts housing and transportation, which will be discussed later. Under the guise of "global warming" carbon output permissions were to be sold to anyone or any industry which pollutes the air by carbon dioxide emissions (the Cap and Trade proposals). Al Gore and others, together with banks like Goldman-Saks, stand to make billions through the gimmick of selling licenses to pollute. Perhaps no more stellar example of the cynical manipulation of misrepresented facts for personal gain could be found anywhere than the idea of global warming through carbon emissions which must be controlled by selling licenses to pollute! Money bends truth for convenience!

Left to innovation and dedicated research by experts in the field, energy will be found and provided, if those with miss-guided concerns and those with an agenda fitted to their drive for wealth and power can be exposed and curtailed.

4. Education.

How are people to be made ready so they can accept the socialist agenda? Let's not forget that this is Fabian Socialism. The socialistic ideals are to be carefully developed over time. And that is precisely what has been and is happening.

Workers are key to socialistic programs. Good workers need job training. Education must become focused upon developing workers who could be effective in production. The old ideas of an education based upon classical moral values has gradually faded away. Who needs Greece and Rome, Aristotle and Plato, Latin or Greek, or Jesus Christ, for that matter?

Classical education, called the humanities, focused upon developing the individual. The Aristotelian model of correct words, plus correct grammar, using sound logic faded into practical communication at the simplest level of language usage. Logic is seldom taught and argumentation changed into persuasive techniques. Since the language with which one speaks is also the language with which one thinks, simple language equals simple thinking; resulting in people incapable of dealing with complicated cause and effect problems. Most modern students can not recognize a fallacy of logic, which makes it easy for socialists to sell their unworkable ideas!

Team work, sports, group endeavors and group sessions of sharing ideas and wishes became central to childhood education (communityism!). What do we want, or what do we think, replaced what we ought to want and what is realistic thinking. Math with its simple structures replaces verbal skills and logic.

Prayer is being removed from schools. History is simplified to exclude the innovators and the important individuals at the expense of how those same people were individuals contributing to the community. Discipline faded into the rights of students at the expense of the truth needed for realistic living. Even "no-grade" classes were tried, in which everyone passes, no one fails. Discipline becomes political correctness rather than dealing with the reality of moral conduct. What is the result?

The goal of Socialist education is a pliable, easily indoctrinated, member of the community who can make an effective contribution in community projects at work and in society. Workers become compliant, non-questioning ciphers in an impersonal system?

The social interaction in the schoolrooms supersedes the family as to the values taught, the skills learned, and the habits inculcated. Children are to report any anti-governmental behavior by their parents or teachers. At the time of entering into adult life, this kind of education should produce a well behaved child, able to be a part of the community, easily persuaded into whatever program or policy the ideologues of government deem are most useful for the "common good!". They are world citizens blending into one cultural image. As indicated above, at this moment students in Superior, Wisconsin, pledge their allegiance to the world rather than to the flag of the United States.

Fabian Socialism has performed very well in reaching its educational goals. In hard learning we rank 37th among the nations of the world by recent tests. Students try to enter college without the ability to read or write. Rebellion is rife in our classrooms and on our streets, fodder for any skilled ideologue. Our students have become ciphers in an impersonal machine designed to turn our good, pliable, future worker bees for the human hive. Who and what they are as an individual will never seem very important to them. What they want, what they can obtain, and the pleasures they seek absorbs their living. Too often they haven't the mental acumen or the self-discipline to make changes in their thinking patterns if they ever encounter other possibilities.

5. Housing.

The idea that some rich people live in mansions while many poor live in shacks is grist for the idea that everyone is equal; everyone should share the wealth of a society. It begins with the principle that there is no private property. No one owns anything. The government owns everything!

As the middle class dwindles, there are only two classes in society—ideologues and bureaucrats who run the government which owns everything, and the workers. Under this system a worker is a worker, whether they are a skilled physician, an inventor, a scholar or a ditch digger. All are paid the same, as regulated by the bureaucrats. Since all have the same wage, all should have the same housing. Hence large apartment complexes are created with so many square feet of living space per person. We shall see how this is implemented by the socialist ideas regarding transportation. Housing complexes of this type are already in the building stage.

Why would anyone agree to go into such living? Poverty! Through taxation, aging, death of the supporting spouse, poor living quality and lack of ambition, one becomes leveled to the place where there is nowhere else to live, governmental housing seems quite welcome. Hyper inflation, due to the failing of the Petrodollar, will make many on fixed incomes look to federal housing as the only alternative.

Universal housing in communal complexes reinforces the educational training of worker's worth. They are a member of a communal society, which has the right to control any errant person who might question or challenge the system. When one's usefulness is ended in old age, they are simply eliminated via death counseling and euthanasia. Communal controlled housing is very important in population control. No more individually designed "man caves!" We shall see how this fits into the ideologue's concept of transportation.

6. Transportation.

The current transportation system of personal cars and large commercial trucks are an anathema to environmentalists, an easy target for Agenda 21 controls by ideologues with their bureaucrats. Remedial steps have already been taken. Federal money is paid to get old "gas guzzlers" out off the road. Electric cars are pushed by Federal subsidies. Gas prices are allowed to rise (except in an election year) to encourage people to use other means of transportation or to limit their trips. Bicycle paths are encouraged.

But a spread out population requires transportation in order to work. Enter federal housing! With people in communities there is little need for a private car. Public transportation and bicycles will do just fine.

Since human transportation involves some degree of air pollution to run the various engines, Agenda 21 people have some very definite ideas concerning cars, trucks, trains and airplanes. They push for research money to build better electric cars. Hybrids are preferred over traditional engines. But a real problem is the trucking industry. Tens of thousands of diesel spouting trucks cruise the highways of the world, emitting pollution, changing the very air we breathe. What to do? Here we have some amazing ideas!

Do not allow any food in the markets of the housing projects that is not locally grown. That means that members of communes in Minnesota will never taste a banana! Members of Pennsylvania communes will never taste salmon! How will Kansas wheat provide flour for the world?

Solution—have electric trains connect the communes. So what will produce the electricity? Renewable energy! Renewable energy sources can at best supply but less than a tenth of the needs for electricity but that is irrelevant to the ideologues! Collective farms will produce all the local food that is needed!

Agricultural production has always been a problem in Socialist societies! If the ploughed and grazing lands are taken away, according to their Biodiversity Assessment Document stated above, where will the food be grown? Workers must eat, but how and what?

This whole fantastic line of reasoning is based upon the belief in global warming. Since our human "carbon footprint" is responsible, control the emissions. Since cars, busses and trucks provide 32% per cent of the carbon emissions, they must be reduced and eventually done away with. Enter electric cars run on electricity produced by wind turbines. Enter bunching the workers in controlled housing, joined by bicycles and public transportation. The unoccupied land will be returned to its biodiversity original. However, if global warming isn't true, the whole reason for this house of cards comes tumbling down.

Now we know why, to prove global warming is due to human carbon imprints, they will distort scientific findings, use any means possible to rush through the Cap and Trade legislation and fabricate by logic-tight reasoning what they cannot prove scientifically. Without the need to control carbon dioxide emissions, no one will make any money selling rights to pollute licenses!

7. Communication

In times past despots tried to prevent the population from gathering and focusing on some form of protest or rebellion by prohibiting freedom of speech and assembly. Without means of interaction, group action was impossible. But in the field of communication we are in a new age of emails and face books, of the radio and television. Information can be dispersed across the nation or across the world in a matter of moments. In this new world, where information cannot be prevented, new forms of control must be devised! To prevent undesirable information from reaching the people three attacks have been launched: Subterfuge so no information is available for transmission to the public, Distortion of information and Demonizing opposing points of view.

The means of the spread of Fabian Socialism is subterfuge, anonymity and simple silence. How many people know about Agenda 21? Of those that have heard of it, how many people have studied to find out what it is all about? Of those who are looking into it, how many people have studied the original Agenda 21 document? We find that this is like that famous quotation about Obamacare, "Pass it and you'll find out what's in it!"

Agenda 21 is in full operation in all policies of the current administration. Ask public officials and many will say they have never heard of it! How was this anonymity accomplished? Deliberately! The population, especially the voters, are deliberately kept from learning about this program. And the news media? Silence! Investigative journalism? Non-existent!

How is this accomplished? George Soros and men like him have controlling interests in all news channels except Fox. Feed the public pap! No news about Agenda 21. No news about how it works or its goals! Hillary Clinton's signing of the U.N. Arms Control directive bans personal firearms; a violation of the 2nd Amendment to our Constitution. This is not news by most news channels, while rescuing a dolphin is! Don't let the populace know! Keep them satisfied with pap!

Distortion of information! For the sake of advancing Agenda 21, Fabian Socialism, lies and half-truths are constantly in use. "I heard that Mitt Romney hasn't filed income taxes for the past ten years!" "My wife died when Mitt Romney closed the factory where I worked and I could no longer get workers compensation hospitalization for her." Over a million dollars have been paid to hide the fact that a Muslim, born in Kenya, is our president. Kagan was awarded as Supreme Court position for her work in hiding Obama's record.

Demonizing the opposition! It's the fault of George Bush, the Republicans and the Fox news channel! The Republicans are pushing grandma in her wheel chair over the cliff! Every attempt is being made to demonize those who oppose the implementation of Agenda 21. Vicious left-wing rhetoric is constantly spewed out through the avenues of television, billboards, radio and mail outs. The rich people hate the middle class and trod on the poor workers. Those who won't save our planet (by our methods) are enemies of mankind. Put them into work camps and reeducate them as the communists do! How can anyone be against saving this or that endangered species? How can anyone be against doing something about global warming?

The problem is the old argument between autocratic and representative government. Autocratic governments, of which Socialism is a prime example, will do anything they can to destroy the arguments and opinions of those who do not agree with them. The classic description was developed by the philosopher Hegel. If John and Mike are equal in status, the decisions they arrive at will tend to be better than when John so dominates Mike that John's decisions are what will be implemented. The ideologues are the Johns and we are the Mikes and the result is evident!

Representative governments assume that everyone is more or less equal. With an equal playing field and honest discussion, the decisions arrived at will be better than if an ideologue tells the populace what to do! Discussions which lead to good decisions require information and the communication of that information, openly, completely and without demonizing those with other ideas. That is precisely what the proponents of Agenda 21 seek to prevent. They have the program, they have the knowledge, so why discuss it? It is a waste of time and only gets in the road of getting programs done! Thank God we have the means today of spreading truth, the whole truth and nothing but the truth if we have the courage to buck the socialist system!

8. Population

There are those who look at the burgeoning population of this world and perceive one answer—reduce it! How? You won't find the advocates of population reduction volunteering to set the example by being the first to go! Ideologues advocate the policies at work in China: abortion, death counseling and laws for "the people!" We are back at the solution for all problems: laws, Blue Helmets to enforce the laws, bureaucrats to administer the solutions and a well-paid ideologue to take credit for the solution. It is suggested by some that the population of the United States be reduced by at least a hundred million and the population of the world be reduced by half. Whatever the numbers and whatever the program, the answer, according to Agenda 21, is less people.

But is there a law or a policy that is going to work worldwide, let alone among male and female couples? Abortions are murder, contraceptives unacceptable by some religions, some desert societies still harbor the idea that a large family is something to be proud of even in that inhospitable climate, some welfare programs are so set up that recipients get more money by having more babies! So what to do? Education! But regardless of what one was taught to believe in, will that belief be in focus in the marriage bed?

Perhaps the truth of the Jesus Message of the worth of every human as over against having children that cannot be cared for, will not have the necessary food and shelter for their development and will exist in standards of living unsuitable for anyone, especially for children, will be realized little by little. Will the mothers of the world take charge and slowly steer the ships of a society into workable channels?

We know that dehumanizing humanity into ciphers on a demographic chart is the worst of all courses to take. It numbs the best of our human spirit. Who has the right to say this person and not that? After the murders, what is left for the murderers?

9. Environment

This is the lever used by the proponents of Agenda 21 in all their propositions. We must save the planet! The question is for what purpose?

Socialism has made their response to these questions very clear. Humans exist as ciphers in the larger plan of workers and the ideologues who guide the workers. The middle class is gone.

The agenda of entrepreneurs planning an enterprise, procuring the means of making that enterprise possible, selling the produced product and experiencing success or failure in that enterprise, no longer exists. It is replaced by bureaucrats who determine what might be, obtaining governmental permission to proceed with the enterprise, passing the governmental examinations, and paying exorbitant taxes from whatever profit derived from the enterprise. The entrepreneur is but a cog in the milieu of Communityisn, Biodiversity and Sustained Development. That is the formula of Agenda 21. That is the program underway even as this is read.

PART FOUR

Problems hindering the implementation of Agenda 21

Those who would implement Agenda 21 run into at least five problems: religion, personal weapons, war mongers, individualism and communication. These five problems must be dealt with or Agenda 21 cannot be implemented. Let us begin with religion.

1. Religion.

All religions deal with one form or another of a relationship with a Deity which transcends and limits human behavior. Christianity, in its original form, is very absolute. There is but one God, one set of rules, which must be obeyed if one is to live well in this Creation. Jesus put it bluntly, "Render to Caesar the things that are Caesar's and to God the things that are God's." (Matthew 22:21)

According to Jesus, there are regions of behavior where the state cannot demand allegiance. Final allegiance belongs to the Deity. That is anathema to socialists! To an ideology which demands total control and absolute obedience to the dictates of the state, Christianity is a bitter pill which must be dealt with, by murder if necessary, by the subterfuge of Fabian Socialism if possible.

The key is the Ten Commandments, the shortened statements of Natural Law. What is to direct behavior, government or the revelations of God? Therefore, in order for Agenda 21 to work, the Ten Commandments must be eliminated, the Christian holidays must be turned into secular holidays and public prayer forbidden. That is the purpose of all the hullabaloo by the American Civil Liberties Union (ACLU). Notice the innocent "civil liberties." The real name should be the American Socialist Order Society (ASOS). Fabian Socialism works to eliminate Christianity via education and secular laws.

It is amazing how little the ideologues understand fundamental Christianity. It will never be eliminated by force. That has been attempted many times—by Rome, the Orient, and in modern communist states to mention a few of hundreds of programs to get rid of Christian ideals. Christianity was alive and vital during the worst of the Soviet purges.

The original Message of Jesus established a personal love bond with any individual who wishes to live His Way of Life through love. Once someone has found that love-bond and the glories of a love-led life, they will gladly suffer martyrdom rather than reject that way of life.

The various socialists have tried to deal with this phenomena by a watered down or "progressive" Christianity which no longer talks about the Ten Commandments or the Jesus commandment to love one another as He loved them. Today one can attend many churches on any Sunday and never hear the Ten Commandments, the Lord's Prayer or the Apostle's Creed! There is an attempt to merge Christianity with Islam into Chrislam. Christianity is a love-bonded relationship with a personal living and all powerful God. Anything less is not the Message Jesus brought from Heaven to Earth. So the power struggle continues between those who will remain faithful to God's Message in Jesus Christ, which works, and the secularism of Socialism, which doesn't and has never worked! Christianity as Jesus taught it, will never fade into the woodwork! There will always be people who have found such love and peace in the Jesus Message that they will suffer martyrdom rather than give it up.

2. The problem of personal weaponry.

The Constitution of the United States expressly guarantees the right of the citizens to own guns and to meet together as a citizen's militia. How the proponents of Agenda 21 have teemed up with "concerned citizens" (read useful fools!) to limit and eventually ban all firearms under the pretext that it will stop crime! If they can't buck it through congress they will try via the United Nations! We are back at probation again! Will we ever learn that as prohibition didn't work gun laws won't either?

As drunkenness increased under prohibition, crime increases when a citizenry is deprived of any means of defense. The entire gun issue is but a smoke screen of the socialists to get people to allow the ban on all forms of citizen self defense so that there will be no effective opposition to their edicts.

Every time there is a violent crime carried out by some gun wielding outlaw, the anti-gun lobby rises again. As with environmentalism, gun control "for the common good," is but a mask to get through some authoritative state the banishment of personal weapons. Socialists want a disarmed citizenry unable to resist the dictates of the ideologues! The real issue is control of everyone. Someone with a gun who might resist having some ideologue's useful fools attempting to disarm them!

Germany in the 1930s was powerless to resist the National Socialist Workers Party. The citizens had few weapons. In Britain today, guns are outlawed. Did that stop crime? Look at the record. Crime has soared in Britain. Recently an elderly man shot a burglar and wounded another. The man was arrested and given a life sentence for murder! The wounded burglar is suing that man for damages!

Advocates of Agenda 21 dare not allow guns in the hands of workers but at the same time they cannot prevent crimes against the unarmed populace. "The police can take care of crime" is a bad joke. By the time the police arrive the perpetrators of the crime are long gone. At least people with guns can defend themselves against criminals but the price is some irresponsible person obtaining weapons and perpetrating a crime. The question seems to be, "Do we want crooks only to have guns and crime soar, or will we allow citizens to have guns with the attendant reality that someone may commit an outrage? Our founding fathers trusted the citizenry more than the crooks! Guns can no more be controlled that alcohol! Anyone who so desires can obtain a weapon capable of killing. The purpose of all this hullabaloo is governmental control of disarmed citizens, under the excuse of preventing crime through banning weapons.

3. <u>The problem of war mongers.</u>

Socialist ideologues believe that everyone wants a just and equitable society—that everyone will work to make it so. The truth is that many people resent having to follow the dictates of government especially if they run counter to self-centered greed, obtaining power, having the means of pleasurable but immoral behavior or simply being told what to do. There is the problem of evil.

Evil is defined as behavior contrary to the patterns of Natural Law—what doesn't work on the long run in this creation as it is made. The philosopher Immanuel Kant spoke of a Categorical Imperative, which asks the question, "What if everybody did it?"

What if everyone stole whatever they wanted? What if everyone lied when it was convenient? What if everyone murdered any person that got into their way? What if sex were free and obtainable for anyone so desiring?

Carried further: Is every leader in a society going to be nice, gentle, working for the good of others when by coercion they can get whatever they want? There are people who are war mongers! It makes little difference if they have much power or little. The question is the use of that power. Many are willing to use the Blue Helmets to enforce by coercion what they say is for the good of the people! What if the Blue Helmets are on the side of the dictator? How can a disarmed citizenry do anything about that?

There is evil in this world. We experience it as a desire to do what doesn't work in harmony with Natural Law. People are tempted to do what the whole of society cannot do if there is to be any semblance of order. If coercion is the only answer, what happens when someone else has the means of coercion—another ideologue differing somewhat from other ideologues? What would prevent the world from becoming as described in Orwell's novel "1984;"–perpetual war for the perpetual profits of wars? Give a Narcissistic Personality Disorder person power and the boundaries of morality, as in the Ten Commandments, will be bent to fulfill the demagogue's wishes. Anything can be done with the excuse that it is for the good of the people! NPD people always sound so convincing!

Socialism has no answer to the problem of evil except more coercion; which always leads to frustration, anger, hostility, divisions and conflicts in all human groupings, whether in a family or in a society. Too many ideologues will use weaponry to impose their wishes on people, the only real restraint is the weaponry of the populace. That takes us to another problem of socialists encounter, the human drive for individuality.

4. The Problem of individualism

It is a fact that every human is different from every other human. Genetic makeup, family environment, experiences, personal health, attitudes, hurts and personal disasters guarantee the uniqueness of every human. As mentioned above, Socialism, and religions such as Buddhism, strive to wipe out individualism. The operative word is Communityism—if everyone is like everyone else society will be safe and secure.

Christianity strives to develop the individual within the confines of moral law, rather than political law. We are to learn how to be creatures of love, joy, peace, kindness and self discipline by practicing those virtues. Because of our uniqueness the expressions of these virtues will vary, but the product is a varied and universal society in which everyone tries to fulfill the larger moral goals.

Christianity attempts to guide our human personalities into positive moral behavior patterns. The human goal of Agenda 21 is a compliant person able to be an effective worker in society. He or she is to be obedient, a community oriented person who never causes any trouble the Blue Helmets cannot handle. When they are no longer useful, there is euthanasia. Life is focused upon serving "Mother Dia," the planet.

It all comes down to our view of humanity. Are we worker bees in a hive of humanity? That is the concept of Socialism. The new aristocrats, the ideologues, live differently. Theirs is the wealth, the pleasure, the power that comes with being part of the new order. Someone must do the thinking for the masses!

Natural Law, as expressed in Christian behavior when the fellowship of believers was first launched two thousand years ago, is built upon an individual relationship of love, a love-bond with God and what God represents. That love bond produces the virtues of love, joy, peace, patience, kindness, goodness, faithfulness, gentleness and self-discipline. After a life time of learning how to live by the Jesus example (loving one another as He loved us) we are graduated into an environment that will fulfill what we have already experienced in part while living in our physical bodies—the ability to live in the fellowship of God in an existence based upon love. So different! Why would anyone choose the Socialist way when they can have the joy and beauty of the Way of Life through love as Jesus lived and taught?

5. The problem of personal means of communication.

As indicated above, until recently all the autocrat had to do to control people was keep them isolated, unable to communicate with one another and thereby arrive at some concerted action. Email, Facebook and the internet changed all that. The Committees of Correspondence which formed the resistance, which led to the American Revolution, took time. Travel between the colonies was slow. Not any more.

The absurdities, and lies, the plans for enforcing details of Agenda 21 can be recognized, identified and dealt with. No more anonymity! This is a crippling blow to Fabian Socialism. So what can the ideologues do?

Surveillance! If the key troublemakers are known, then they can be gotten rid of by one means or another. Drones are in use at this moment to survey land use, gatherings of people and the flow of traffic.

A special drone has been developed by the FBI and the CIA. These Cyborg Insect Drones are called MAVs, for micro air vehicle. They are very small, three centimeters in size. They can fly through open doorways and windows, photograph and transmit what it sees and even take a DNA sample of blood. The Air Force funds research for this new surveillance tool at John Hopkins University and the University of Pennsylvania.

Perhaps the most immediately pressing issue is the so-called "smart meters." Every user of electricity is to have one. They are to simplify bookkeeping by radio transmission of who and what electricity is used. They can also be used to control the amount of electricity used! They can also transmit whatever is going on in the house. Perfect surveillance tool! Submit or you get no electricity!

Apart from the surveillance, there is a health problem. Electronic impulses strong enough to transmit to a central collecting tower can cause all manner of health issues. What difference does that make to a government which must know what its citizens are doing!

Information must be collected and made ready for analysis. Enter the computer. By this means a data base can be easily assembled for every person living in the United States.

But still those emails and the internet! Attempts have been made to control the satellite emissions, to regulate email and to "license" cell phones—anything to control the transmission of information! So far nothing is final but the ideologues will not rest until they will know every word said by each and every person. They who can control the information can control the people. Lack of not being able to do this has really crippled the anonymity of the Agenda 21 implementation. The ability to expose various programs and plans has developed 21st Century Committees of Correspondence who are using the internet to expose the perpetrators of Agenda 21.

PART FIVE

What we can do?

I shall treat this Part Five under four headings: Information, communication, recognition and action.

<u>Information.</u>
Just as Fabian Socialism seeks to hide its activities, in this case behind the green mask of environmentalism, so the antidote is exposure. What would people do if they really understood what Agenda 21 is and how it will impact their lives? There might be some lynching!

When one first learns about Agenda 21, and it means of implementation, the first reaction is disbelief. "This will never happen in the good old U.S.A." But it is happening! It is in process at this moment through the Czars and the Executive Orders of the current administration. It is called "Biosurveilance." Billions of dollars are dedicated by this administration for its implementation.

We must know the programs, how they are being put into practice, the lies behind which Agenda 21 hides and the ultimate goal of the ideologues and their stooges. We must know that this is put into practice by baby steps. Too big a step and we would wake up! Don't turn the heat up too fast under the frog! We must never use the excuse that "people wouldn't do something like that to their fellow humans!" People can be found who will do anything and obey anyone, for money, and power. Hitler had no problem finding soldiers who would operate his death camps!

We must spread the message everywhere, not as alarmists, but as citizens who do not want to be part of this system. Certainly we will encounter skeptics, misinformation and downright lies but truth in love is the strongest weapon in this Creation.

Communication.

There are many Tea Party type activists who are aware of the deadly dangers of Agenda 21. Join them. Use Email. Learn what is going on and spread the truth. Above all, identify the lies, the misrepresentations and the hidden agenda behind the green mask. Every time we buy into a misrepresentation we advance this program for the enslavement of people, ourselves!

Recognition.

Here is where our "politically correctness" has really crippled us. Too many people believe that although other people have different ideas, but in the need for us to get along, why rock the boat? Let them do their thing and I'll do mine and we'll all get along! Political correctness!

We forget one thing—Natural Law. If we know anything about our world through the scientific studies of the last three centuries, we know that this world operates on fixed laws, one set of laws, and they are in force everywhere and in all of time. These laws are not passed by any legislature, they don't exist, or not exist, by the decrees of some autocrat and do not change from one place in time to another. THIS IS REALITY regardless of how many humans may think otherwise. Every science has thick books within their disciplines of the rules by which this Creation operates, whether chemistry, physics, astronomy, psychology or economics, biology or anthropology. It is a sad irony that in the midst of more knowledge than the human race has ever possessed, there are those who don't believe there are consequences for breaking Natural Law. They can` treat relationships, the environment or their bodies however they wish without consequences! Amazing!

Let us say it again: <u>Every act that any human does has consequences</u>. It is common sense! This has nothing to do with whether we believe it or not. There is nothing anyone can do to change the lightest decree of it! Reality <u>is</u> reality!

When human religions enter the picture, do they deal with this reality or are they concerned with keeping some Deity happy, as explained by some priesthood for the benefit of that priesthood? There is no more spectacular failure in human religions than right here. We need to know the rules and the consequences as expressed in Natural Law in the Ten Commandments. No religion made them up—they are whether we believe in them or not. The Ten Commandments are but a simplified and abbreviated version of Natural Law. (1) There is but one set of rules. (2) Don't change the rules by human invention. (3) Don't count God's decrees as nothing. (4) Take time out for spiritual matters. (5) Honor those who have journeyed well in their living. (6) Do not murder for life is precious. (7) Do not commit sexual sins for the family is essential for the well being of society. (8) Do not steal. (9) Do not lie. (10) Do not envy or try to appropriate what is another's.

It is so silly, this attempt to remove the Ten Commandments from walls and courtrooms. They are, whether we believe in them or not! Since they are, hadn't we better take a look at them from time to time?

Those who feel called to deal with spiritual matters must realize that their duty is to explain Natural Law as expressed in the Ten Commandments. No compromise! No political correctness! Anything less that this simple truth is a lie. Political correctness is a lie!

Once we realize the absolute nature of the Law, then we can realize that we have broken the Law and the consequence is death—absolutely and unequivocally! Here Jesus enters the picture. He did two things: He lived and taught us how to practice the laws of righteousness through love and He was the Sacrificial Lamb taking on Himself the consequences of our sins. We stand in Jesus as though we had never sinned; therefore we follow the Good Shepherd into learning how to practice a love-based life following the commandment of Jesus, "Love one another as I have loved you." (John 13:34, 15:12, 17)

So we have the two covenants, the Law which says we must live in harmony with Natural law or die, and the Gospel which gives us a new relationship with God so that we can by practicing it, learn how to live a life motivated and undergirded by a life based upon love—a love which cares, which responds to real needs, which respects the individual and understands life's situations. While this has not been always realized or practiced, this is the Jesus message which He lived and taught.

This is diametrically opposed to the goals and programs of Agenda 21. Let us examine this difference by the nine issues listed in Part Three.

Control of the Means of production. Are governmental bureaucrats better able to assemble the means of economic growth through government permits, licenses and inspectors looking for deviations from some ideologues idea of how it must be, or by an entrepreneur with a plan, assembling the means of production, marketing his or her idea and reaping profits or failure from the endeavor? Which makes better use of the Natural Laws of this creation and the human spirit's strive to excel? Is one better motivated by love of one's work or by coercion?

Medicine. Medicine is needed to help people through difficult times. Is that medicine better administrated by people directed by impersonal medical teams or by people who care, respond to real need, respect the integrity of the patient and understand what it needed by a heart-felt commitment? Is the purpose of medicine to keep the workers working and then terminating the worker's life when they are no longer needed or to minister to real needs in a sympathetic and understanding manner? Which better promotes healing?

Energy. Why go through all the problems of providing energy for human needs? We have provided power grids, petroleum distillation factories, manufacturers for making tools, home furnishings, and the myriad of other products using energy, especially the automotive industry. Why? Is it to perpetuate some ideologue's idea of society or to fulfill human needs which lead to better quality of living for individuals? The focus of the ideologues of Agenda 21 is a compliant, well organized and working mechanism called the community. The focus of Christianity is to fulfill the human innate drives for love, joy, peace and beauty and by the individual growing up into a fulfillment of these virtues he or she is better able to serve the community. The energy needed to fulfill human needs—is it better used for an impersonal social machine led by oughtnesses directed for the welfare of the autocrats, or directed by that which allows the flow of energy to develop fulfillments of the dreams of individual entrepreneurs under Natural Law?

Education. Here we come to another real parting of the ways between Socialism and Christianity. Socialism wants to develop a person who is a well fitting cog in the communal arena. Christianity wants to develop the individual into the fullness of his or her potential which then allows them to build a better society through their unique contribution. Socialism uses coercion to achieve its goals. Christianity uses the motivation of love.

Which system promotes the better guide for living? For what are we educating our youth, to be better workers in a machine or to deeper living through a life based on the Jesus Commandment, "Love one another as I have loved you?"

Are we giving our children the gifts which lead to better living; the ability to think, to understand reality and logically deal with the information they receive? The Aristotelian process of correct words in correct grammatical form guided by logic is anathema to the socialists. Forbid the possibility of the citizen capable of thinking for themselves! Think like the herd, directed by self-centered bureaucrats led by self-centered ideologues! That is supposed to produce the ideal society!

Housing. What is a house? Something to protect one from the weather? A man or woman centered cave? A retreat from the world?

What happens to attitudes when people are all packed together over a period of time? We are individuals and our individuality is best served with housing that fits our person. The Natural Law of this creation illustrates what happens when plants or animals are crowded together! We humans need space if we are to reach our individual potential.

Who knows what is best, a bureaucrat with his or her computer, or the person wishing to live in that house? No where is the controlling mechanism of socialists more in evidence then in its idea of how to house the workers. Their ideal is illustrated by a bee hive. What does that do to the development of the individual?

Once again the socialist ideal of communityism takes center stage. Socialism seeks compliant workers, each in their prescribed cell, each working for the "common good" as determined by the governing bureaucrats. That is supposed to lead to human welfare! In the Socialist system there are only two classes, the bureaucrats led by the ruling autocrats in their mansions, and the workers in their prescribed cells, all owned by the government!

Transportation. Since the purpose of the workers is to work the various machines through their labor, they must eat. Food and other products not locally grown or manufactured must be trucked in! Trucking creates environmental problems. So get rid of the trucks by eating only what is locally grown. Electric trains will provide whatever transportation is needed between communities, and electric streetcars, bicycle paths and pedestrian lanes will serve the transportation needs within communities.

Workers will live out their lives in a small, intimate and comfortable community boxes. There is no need for new ideas, wider horizons or varied experiences. Why travel when all one needs is immediately available? Security at a price!

The Jesus version of Christianity constantly invites the individual to new and broader horizons. One's adult life is designed to be an ever widening expanse of experiences resulting in spiritual and physical development. Which develops the better human, someone who desires to use their opportunities to grow and develop throughout their lifetime or someone hunkered down in a comfortable box?

Communication. Since the role of communication under Agenda 21 is control of the populace, only those ideas which further the designs of the ideologue autocrat are permitted. They who control the information can control the individuals. But to what end? A more compliant worker? Is that all an individual can expect—work, control, community and euthanasia?

The Jesus Way invites discussion, understanding and new information. It assumes that we never know all that we can use for better living. Although dogmatism has sometimes plagued the Christian world, that is a human failing. "You shall know the truth and the truth shall set you free," Jesus said. How shall we recognize that truth? Truth must conform to the revelations of God as given by the Holy Spirit—what conforms to the rules of Creation, as in Natural Law and the Ten Commandments, and to the life and teachings of Jesus, is truth. No wonder socialists want to get rid of the Ten Commandments!

We approach God's revelations by being humble, being teachable, as in the first of the Beatitudes. (Matthew 5:3) Again the focus is upon the well developed individual. By using their developed particular gifts, Christians practicing the Jesus Way make the best contribution to society—far better than compliant workers living comfortably in their little boxes. Will the interaction of our communication direct us into narrow coercion channels or into ever widening vistas of awarenesses?

Population. The Jesus Way of Life through love focuses on the family. Close-knit, loving and disciplined families produce individuals capable of realizing their potential. Anything that minimizes that potential is evil, ultimately working for the short-circuiting of their natural development. Fornication, adultery or homosexuality are obvious violations of Natural Law. But so is a child reared by the state in ideas which must conform to the going political ideas as presented by the ideological aristocrats.

We are individuals. We are so by the Natural Laws of genetics, environments and learning. Will the family produce better individuals under the morality of Natural law based upon love, or do we give the children over to being wards of the state, which will supervise all stages of their development into a compliant, disciplined and community centered worker?

Population control by abortion, death counseling and euthanasia is simply not part of a Deity of life, who is obviously a biophiliac. Christianity focuses on the quality of love-bonded families as over against indoctrinated children as wards of the state. Again, the ideal is the development of the uniqueness of the individual as over against producing worker bees to serve some ideological "Queen."

Environment. We finally come to the nub of the matter. We do live in this world, in a particular environment and in a world setting. But why? Why do we exist; to serve as cogs in a machine manufactured and sustained by Blue Helmets or to develop our own particular uniqueness into the fulfillment of that specialness? What do we do with uniqueness? Socialist would rub it off, produce a compliant worker serving an autocratic bureaucracy. Christianity believes in a moral universe where Natural Law functions both as a reward for harmony and as a warning for rebellion. Within those parameters the individual is to develop into his or her uniqueness.

So is the environment to serve the goal of the autocrat or the needs of the individual? Will proponents of environmental programs advocate suggestions to be debated or decrees to be implemented according to some ideological autocrat? Which produces the better society, one based upon coercion or one based upon love, respect and the joy of achievement?

We have compared Socialism, as advanced in Agenda 21, and the Jesus version of Christianity. It is obvious that the two systems are absolutely opposed to one another. There is no middle ground between a system based upon releasing and using the individual drive for achievement and the system in which the ideologue enforces absolute control through coercion to achieve a two system society—the workers and the "queens." Either we have a moral society based upon Natural Law, which is expressed in the Ten Commandments, motivated by the Jesus type of love, or we can have a society in which the morals are determined by an ideological autocrat and carried out by coercion.

In Christian theology this conflict goes much deeper. It involves evil, which is defined as "that which doesn't work in this creation on the long run." Socialism is a system which has never worked, yet is loudly proclaimed by its advocates. Why? Why should millions of people be killed to bring about an economic and social system which has never worked, as in Russia, China, Cambodia, Cuba? How about Fabian Socialism as in the European Union? They are about to drown in their own mismanagement!

Why doesn't everyone adopt the Gospel of Jesus Christ, which has worked every time it is tried, both in personal lives and in the society touched by those lives. We all know the reason. Too many people who say they are Christians neither obey the Law nor do they practice the Jesus Commandment of loving one another as He loved us.

Once people know true Christianity by witnessing it in practice, they are sometimes ready to consider it as a life style.

What the world has witnessed is a succession of priests, ministers and self-proclaimed leaders of worship centers who are hypocrites, living well off the gifts of people. Their list of crimes go from child molestation, to homosexuality, to being willing to say from the pulpit what will support them and keep them in that pulpit. When was the last time you heard the Ten Commandments, or the commandment of Jesus to love one another as He loved us in a church service? Too many people think of false teachers and practitioners when they think of Christianity. Again, we must base our lives upon Natural Law is expressed in the Ten Commandments, motivated by the Jesus Commandment. That is the only alternative to Agenda 21 with the power to oppose and defeat it. It is the only viable alternative to the socialist world of Agenda 21.

So we need to recognize the four tributaries that make up the river Agenda 21: environmental concerns, secular humanism, Socialism and the banking cartels which reap huge profits as the agenda is facilitated. Then we need to also recognize true Christianity, based on Natural Law which is expressed in the Ten Commandments and motivated by the Jesus Way of Life through love. Then we have a true picture of the ongoing battle we live in today. Those are the two sides of the ongoing Battle of Armageddon.

We can speak of the rights of man, of the American Constitution, the Bill of Rights and representative government but we need to realize the foundation of those documents is Natural Law. We can speak of this religion or that, but if they're not based upon Natural Law they are but another human contrivance, another human Tower of Babel. And that is the fundamental weakness of Socialism. It is another human contrivance ignoring Natural Law.

Thomas Paine put it accurately in his "Common Sense." His writings gave simple common sense approaches to the problem of the colonists with Britain. Let's step back and view Agenda 21 with that same dispassionate common sense.

SUMMARY

We are concerned about our environment. We have abused our stewardship of this island home. But we need to look at this situation from the confluence of those other three rivers of thought, secular humanism, Socialism and the Banking Cartels.

Is man the measure of all things? Do I, do we, have in our short span of existence the ability to understand all that is needed to make absolute life and death decisions? Haven't we demonstrated over and over again that man's measurement of anything is biased and self-centered? How can we, the finite understand Infinity? Is it common sense to hand over our decisions to another finite human? Is an anti-social Karl Marx, sitting on his boils in the London Museum going to make decisions upon which to base one's life? Is it true, the saying that "Socialists love humanity but hate people." Is love of people and their need for spiritual development even mentioned in Agenda 21?

Perhaps the muddiest tributary to the river of Agenda 21 is the banking cartels—those who stand to make billions while implementing it. They become the new aristocracy through managing the cash flow necessary for Agenda 21. If Cap and Trade had been passed it is estimated that Al Gore would have received one and a half million dollars a year from the sales of those licenses to pollute! The money moguls are living handsomely off the interest paid to loans made for the prosecution of wars, for the various welfare and entitlement programs and for the money to be made off implementing Agenda 21. Human greed! Money! We have given over the income of our grandchildren to finance what the politicians use to buy votes to keep them in power. Let us keep in mind the vast fortunes made by NGOs for handling the money we tax payers give them to do our work instead of our elected officials—those Private/Public Partnerships.

Bureaucrats are routinely paid far more than they could earn in the private sector.

Is it all a money scheme? Is money and power the motivating force behind the Green Mask? Could a Castro or a Hitler or a Mao or a Stalin or a shareholder in the Federal Reserve System have earned a living in honest work? Look what a disaster each of them have been to the human beings of the world! When are we the people going to say, "Enough!"

Agenda 21 is but a money making scheme intended to install a new world-wide aristocracy of the money moguls, beginning with the Bilderburgs and continuing through our Federal Reserve system, the World Bank, the International Monetary Fund, the Council of Foreign Relations and every czar and bureaucrat living off the life blood of the people.

Jesus spoke of the antichrists to come who would sit in places of power usurping the allegiance that is due to God for their own benefit. (Matthew 24) They build their power on the lie that they will bring needed change. They must do whatever they can to discredit the Message of Jesus. They are human beings with the personal strength of lamb's horns, but they are sustained by the power of evil. (Revelation 13:11-18)

We have what they fear most. Our personal integrity, our human drive for what Jesus has to offer, our physical and spiritual weaponry, our means of communication and men and women willing to give their lives for the betterment of each human being. We are not alone in this struggle. The Creator who placed His love within us will be our guide and strength. History is replete with the men and women, often unsung, who have learned to live lives of righteousness based upon love. Now it is our turn.

New human antichrists have arisen, once more attempting to coerce and control people into becoming a community centered worker bee in an impersonal society. The beauty and the abilities of the individual within moral law must be wiped out. The love-bond between human beings and the Creator and Redeemer must be destroyed. Government is the messiah!

Due to the lure of money and power such Anti-Christs will always be around. But today we have the truth, and the means of spreading that truth, so that men and women who are motivated by love of what might and ought to be can unite to defeat Agenda 21 and all such programs pushed by the arrogance and greed of ideologues. For our own well being, let's be about that which works! We are not alone. The God of this creation still runs the show if He can find individuals who choose to live His Way of Life!

Each person lives their moment in time. We choose, daily, hourly, this not that. And what we choose we become. It is an iron law of this Creation. Every human will make the decisions they believe are needed for their own well being and the welfare of their societies. Too many are willing to surrender this gift of freedom for the security of a defined box. We who live at this time of those four rivers must recognize the situation, together with what will happen if no other choices are made.

What if we changed those four "rivers" into the truth of Christianity as it came into our world nearly two thousand years ago, if we returned to the vision of our founding fathers, if we broke the unholy alliance between the politicians and the financiers, replacing it with men and women who would use money and power for the common good, and if our love for our planet was exercised with truth and understanding.

What would happen if each of us chose what is best for ourselves and our respective societies and walked in love with the gift of life we have been given. Human life and living would then experience a new burst of beauty as it realizes some of its potential. The Great I Am could then guide more people into becoming little "I ams."

Other Books by Dr. Zillmer

The Koran, Jesus Christ and Common Sense

This is not a put down of the Muslim religion but an analytical and objective series of quotations from the teachings of Mohammed in the Koran and the teachings of Jesus in the gospels of Matthew, Mark, Luke and John, placed in common sense juxtaposition.

ISBN #978-1-4500-3165-3, Hardcover
#978-1-4500-3164-6, Softcover
#978-1-4500-3265-0, E-book

The Joys of the Lord
Daily Meditations from the Writings of John

This is a daily inspirational book based upon the Gospel, the Epistles and the Book of Revelation. Jesus said, "These things I have spoken unto you that you may have my joy in yourselves, and your joy may be made full." (John 15:11)

ISBN #978-1-4257-7253-6, Hardcover
#978-1-4257-7251-2, Softcover

Are You My Friend?

This book is based upon the three questions Jesus asked Peter: "Do you love me more than these (things)?" "Are you committed to Me in a marriage-type commitment of love?" "Are you My friend?" This is a study of the First Century Jesus Message as it entered the Gentile world. Subsequent chapters focus on the Jesus Way of Life through love as it encountered various diversions down through the ages; how its triumphant struggles and its crippling distortions are part of our Christian walk today. The book ends with a vision of what could be if we, with Peter, answered affirmatively those three questions and thereby shared the greatest adventure we humans can experience.

ISBN #978-1-4415-4144-4, Hardcover
#978-1-4415-4143-7, Softcover

CPSIA information can be obtained at www.ICGtesting.com
Printed in the USA
LVOW08s0340050813

346252LV00002B/252/P

9 781479 711703